LAURIE BERKNER
PILLOWLAND

ILLUSTRATED BY CAMILLE GAROCHE

Simon & Schuster Books for Young Readers

New York London Toronto Sydney New Delhi

To LDM, BSM, and all the other pillow-fort builders and dreamers—L. B.

For my niece Aurore—C. G.

SIMON & SCHUSTER BOOKS FOR YOUNG READERS

An imprint of Simon & Schuster Children's Publishing Division

1230 Avenue of the Americas, New York, New York 10020

Text copyright © 2011 by Laurie Berkner

Illustrations copyright © 2017 by Camille Garoche

All rights reserved, including the right of reproduction in whole or in part in any form.

SIMON & SCHUSTER BOOKS FOR YOUNG READERS is a trademark of Simon & Schuster, Inc.

For information about special discounts for bulk purchases, please contact Simon & Schuster Special Sales at 1-866-506-1949

or business@simonandschuster.com.

The Simon & Schuster Speakers Bureau can bring authors to your live event. For more information or to book an event, contact

the Simon & Schuster Speakers Bureau at 1-866-248-3049 or visit our website at www.simonspeakers.com.

Book design by Lucy Ruth Cummins

The text for this book is set in Quimbly.

The illustrations for this book are photographs of papercut artwork, with detailing done in Photoshop.

Manufactured in China

0817 SCP

First Edition

2 4 6 8 10 9 7 5 3 1

Library of Congress Cataloging-in-Publication Data

Names: Berkner, Laurie, author. | Garoche, Camille, 1982- illustrator.

Title: Pillowland / Laurie Berkner ; illustrated by Camille Garoche.

Description: First edition. | New York : Simon & Schuster Books for Young Readers, [2017]

Identifiers: LCCN 2016020172 | ISBN 9781481464673 (hardcover : alk. paper) | ISBN 9781481464680 (eBook)

Subjects: LCSH: Children's songs, English—United States—Texts. | CYAC: Pillows—

Songs and music. | Bedtime—Songs and music. | Songs.

Classification: LCC PZ8.3.B4558 Pi 2017 | DDC 782.42 [E]—dc23

LC record available at https://lccn.loc.gov/2016020172

I know a place,
a kingdom far away,

where people wear pajamas
every night and every day.

Where all the houses,
the buildings,
and the trees
are made of fluffy pillows that
are soft as they can be.

Where we can ride a pillow train,
choo choo!

or drive a pillow car,
beep beep!

fly a magic pillow plane,
zoom zoom!

swing on a pillow falling star! wheeeee!

And when we let go,

we'll land in Pillowland!

Land in Pillowland.

A feather ocean

and a blanket boat,

we're riding to a pillow castle

through a quilted moat.

We'll meet the king,

and then we'll meet the queen.

They'll show us all the
pillow secrets

no one else has seen.

Like how to ride a pillow train,

choo choo!

or drive a pillow car,

beep beep!

fly a magic pillow plane,

zoom zoom!

swing on a pillow falling star!

wheeeee!

And when we let go,

we'll land in Pillowland!

Land in Pillowland.

Pillow bread and pillow jam
on pillow dinnerware,

you will find me right

beside you

throwing them in the air!

And then we'll ask the king

just one more thing:

"What do we do at night?"

"We gather up the pillows, and . . .

we have a pillow fight!"

And then we'll land

in Pillowland.

Land in Pillowland.